Dear Parents and Educators,

Welcome to Penguin Young Readers! As parents and educators, you know that each child develops at his or her own pace—in terms of speech, critical thinking, and, of course, reading. Penguin Young Readers recognizes this fact. As a result, each Penguin Young Readers book is assigned a traditional easy-to-read level (1–4) as well as a Guided Reading Level (A–P). Both of these systems will help you choose the right book for your child. Please refer to the back of each book for specific leveling information. Penguin Young Readers features esteemed authors and illustrators, stories about favorite characters, fascinating nonfiction, and more!

The Barker Twins™: Boss for a Day

LEVEL **2**

GUIDED READING LEVEL **I**

This book is perfect for a **Progressing Reader** who:
- can figure out unknown words by using picture and context clues;
- can recognize beginning, middle, and ending sounds;
- can make and confirm predictions about what will happen in the text; and
- can distinguish between fiction and nonfiction.

Here are some **activities** you can do during and after reading this book:
- Character Traits: Morgie and Moffie are twins, but they each have their own character traits. Make a list of words that describe Morgie. Make a list of words that describe Moffie.
- Compare/Contrast: Look at the list you made for Morgie and Moffie. How are the twins alike? How are they different?
- Make Predictions: How do you think Morgie felt when Moffie was bossing him around? How would you feel if you were Moffie?

Remember, sharing the love of reading with a child is the best gift you can give!

—Bonnie Bader, EdM
 Penguin Young Readers program

D0104830

*Penguin Young Readers are leveled by independent reviewers applying the standards developed by Irene Fountas and Gay Su Pinnell in *Matching Books to Readers: Using Leveled Books in Guided Reading*, Heinemann, 1999.

For all the "Bosses" in my life, especially
Doug, Bob, Maureen, Judie, Margaret, Jane,
Cecilia, Katrina, Jenny, and Mario,
but not Sally Campbell.

Jennifer Smith-Stead, Literacy Consultant

Penguin Young Readers
Published by the Penguin Group
Penguin Group (USA) Inc., 375 Hudson Street, New York, New York 10014, USA
Penguin Group (Canada), 90 Eglinton Avenue East, Suite 700, Toronto, Ontario M4P 2Y3, Canada
(a division of Pearson Penguin Canada Inc.)
Penguin Books Ltd., 80 Strand, London WC2R 0RL, England
Penguin Group Ireland, 25 St. Stephen's Green, Dublin 2, Ireland (a division of Penguin Books Ltd.)
Penguin Group (Australia), 250 Camberwell Road, Camberwell, Victoria 3124, Australia
(a division of Pearson Australia Group Pty. Ltd.)
Penguin Books India Pvt. Ltd., 11 Community Centre, Panchsheel Park, New Delhi—110 017, India
Penguin Group (NZ), 67 Apollo Drive, Rosedale, Auckland 0632, New Zealand
(a division of Pearson New Zealand Ltd.)
Penguin Books (South Africa) (Pty.) Ltd., 24 Sturdee Avenue,
Rosebank, Johannesburg 2196, South Africa

Penguin Books Ltd., Registered Offices: 80 Strand, London WC2R 0RL, England

Copyright © 2001 by Tomie dePaola. All rights reserved. First published in 2001 by Grosset & Dunlap,
an imprint of Penguin Group (USA) Inc. THE BARKER TWINS is a trademark of Penguin Group (USA) Inc.
Published in 2012 by Penguin Young Readers, an imprint of Penguin Group (USA) Inc.,
345 Hudson Street, New York, New York 10014. Manufactured in China.

Library of Congress Control Number: 2001055628

ISBN 978-0-448-42544-3   1 0 9 8 7 6 5 4 3 2

PENGUIN YOUNG READERS

LEVEL **2**
PROGRESSING READER

THE BARKER TWINS™

BOSS FOR A DAY

by Tomie dePaola

Penguin Young Readers
An Imprint of Penguin Group (USA) Inc.

MOFFAT · 1:02 P.M.   MORGAN · 1:12 P.M.

Moffie liked being the boss.

After all, she was 10 minutes

older than Morgie.

"Morgie, don't wear that shirt,"

Moffie said.

"Wear this one."

"Morgie, you are always

reading that book,"

Moffie said.

"Try this one."

"Morgie, we are going to play

school now," Moffie said.

"I am the teacher.

You and Dolly are the class."

"But I don't want to play school,"

Morgie said.

Mama heard Moffie.

"You are being too bossy,"

she told Moffie.

"Let Morgie do what he wants."

Moffie thought about it.

At bedtime Moffie said,

"Morgie, I have a good idea.

Tomorrow you be the boss."

"But I don't know how,"

Morgie said.

"It is easy," Moffie said.

"I will show you.

Now go to sleep."

The next morning,

Moffie woke up Morgie.

"Get up, Morgie," Moffie said.

"It's time to be the boss."

Moffie picked up two skirts.

"Should I wear my blue skirt

or my pink skirt?" she asked.

Before Morgie said a word,

Moffie said, "I will wear my

pink skirt."

Morgie and Moffie

sat down at the table

for breakfast.

"Morgie," Moffie said,

"you have to tell me

to drink my milk!"

"Drink your milk," Morgie said.

"Do you want muffins or toast?"

Mama asked the twins.

"We want toast, Mama,"

Morgie said.

"No," Moffie said.

"We want muffins."

After breakfast,

Moffie asked Morgie,

"What are we going to do today?"

Morgie got his dinosaurs.

"Let's play," Morgie said.

"That is no fun," Moffie said.

She got Dolly.

"Now let's play."

So they did.

After lunch,

Billy came over.

"Morgie is the boss today,"

Moffie told Billy.

"We have to do everything he says."

"Let's play jump rope,"
Moffie said.

They played
jump rope.

"Let's play Follow the Leader,"

Moffie said.

They played Follow the Leader.

They played dress-up.

"Now let's have a tea party,"

Moffie said.

"I have to go home,"

Billy said.

At supper,

Moffie told Papa,

"Morgie was the boss *all* day.

I did everything he told me to.

Right, Morgie?"

After their baths, the twins
got ready for bed.

"I had so much fun today, Morgie,"

Moffie said.

"See? I told you it was easy to be

the boss!"

But Morgie didn't hear Moffie.

He was fast asleep.

Wow! Moffie thought,

being BOSS really wore him out.